PUFFIN BOOKS

LUKE LANCELOT
AND THE TREASURE OF THE KINGS

Giles Andreae is an award-winning
children's author and has written both fiction
titles and bestselling picture books. He is
probably most famous as the creator of the
phenomenally successful Purple Ronnie,
Britain's favourite stickman. Giles lives
in London and Cornwall with his wife and
three young children.

Puffin books by Giles Andreae

Young fiction
LUKE LANCELOT AND THE GOLDEN SHIELD

LUKE LANCELOT AND THE TREASURE OF THE KINGS

Picture books
CAPTAIN FLINN AND THE PIRATE DINOSAURS

Luke Lancelot

and the Treasure of the Kings

Giles Andreae

Illustrated by Tony Ross

PUFFIN

To Dylan and Charly

PUFFIN BOOKS

Published by the Penguin Group
Penguin Books Ltd, 80 Strand, London WC2R 0RL, England
Penguin Group (USA) Inc., 375 Hudson Street, New York, New York 10014, USA
Penguin Group (Canada), 10 Alcorn Avenue, Toronto, Ontario, Canada M4V 3B2
(a division of Pearson Penguin Canada Inc.)
Penguin Ireland, 25 St Stephen's Green, Dublin 2, Ireland (a division of Penguin Books Ltd)
Penguin Group (Australia), 250 Camberwell Road, Camberwell, Victoria 3124, Australia
(a division of Pearson Australia Group Pty Ltd)
Penguin Books India Pvt Ltd, 11 Community Centre, Panchsheel Park, New Delhi – 110 017, India
Penguin Group (NZ), cnr Airborne and Rosedale Roads, Albany, Auckland 1310, New Zealand
(a division of Pearson New Zealand Ltd)
Penguin Books (South Africa) (Pty) Ltd, 24 Sturdee Avenue, Rosebank, Johannesburg 2196, South Africa

Penguin Books Ltd, Registered Offices: 80 Strand, London WC2R 0RL, England

www.penguin.com

First published 2005
1

Text copyright © Giles Andreae, 2005
Illustrations copyright © Tony Ross, 2005
All rights reserved

The moral right of the author and illustrator has been asserted

Set in 14.25/20pt MT Perpetua
Made and printed in England by Clays Ltd, St Ives plc

British Library Cataloguing in Publication Data
A CIP catalogue record for this book is available from the British Library

ISBN 0–141–31657–8

CONTENTS

It was the dead of night. A pale, silver moon hung in the cloudless sky.

Slowly, silently, a long, narrow boat was gliding across a lake, its dark water unruffled and still as glass.

A low mist hung above the surface and, through the mist, strange ghost-like shapes were drifting, their eyes dark, empty and hollow.

Above the boat flew four black swans. The boat followed their path, although there were no ropes between them. It was as though there was some

strange magic, perhaps in the air from the beat of their wings, that was propelling the boat below them.

In the middle of the lake was an island. And in the middle of the island loomed a vast, black mountain.

The boat reached the shore of the island and the swans landed gracefully beside it. No sooner had they touched the ground than they began to change shape. They became four tall women, all wearing black cloaks.

They reached into the boat and, very gently, they lifted out a small, hunched figure. She was also dressed in a black cloak with a deep hood that hid her face completely.

'Thank you, my sisters,' she said, stepping on to the shore. 'Soon none of this will matter.' She gestured towards her face. 'Because when I get to the treasure with Pendragon's Belt in my hands . . . I will have the power to live for ever!' She cackled dryly.

'And the person who made this happen to me . . . the person whose wretched family was the cause of all this . . . will pay!' She turned to the four women. 'Go now!' she commanded. 'I have work to do.'

The women changed back into black swans and took flight away from the island. The boat followed behind them, drawn by their strange magic, towards the far shore.

As the fragile figure watched them go, she pulled back the hood of her cloak and the moon lit up her face. It was a hideous sight. The skin hung in craggy folds from her bony cheeks, scarred with dark, shiny burns. Her hair was fused in a coarse, messy knot to the back of her head and a scorched eyelid hung like a flap, half-closed over a black, eyeless socket.

'Oh yes, believe me,' she croaked. 'You'll pay for this . . . Luke Lancelot!'

1. TREASURE AT HOME

Luke and his older brother, Arthur, couldn't
wait to get out of the car. It had been a hot day
and they hated going shopping with their
mother. Gwinnie, their younger sister, had
been more helpful in the supermarket but she
too was thankful when the car drew up outside
their house and the children could all finally
scramble out.

'Gwinnie, you've got a party tomorrow,'
said their mother. 'Let's all have supper and get
an early night so you can really enjoy it. It's

been a long day.'

'Are you still going as Queen Guinevere?' Arthur asked.

'Of course!' said Gwinnie with a smile.

'You always go as Guinevere.'

'Well, you never stop pretending that you're a knight with that sword of yours, either,' answered Gwinnie.

'The sword of a brave knight!' Arthur said. He had been given a real, ancient sword on his last birthday and he treasured it more than anything else he owned.

'Girls can be brave too, Arthur,' said their mother. 'Sometimes braver,' she added with a sigh. 'Why don't you go and put your costume together now, Gwinnie?' she went on. 'You boys can help me unload the car.'

'Oh, Muuum,' moaned Luke.

'Come on, Luke,' said Arthur. 'There's a lot of shopping in there and I'm hungry. The sooner we get it out, the sooner we can eat!'

'Good point,' said Luke, and the boys set to work.

'Spaghetti Bolognese?' suggested their mother once all the shopping was in the house.

'Yes, please,' replied Arthur and Luke eagerly.

In no time, the spaghetti was on the boil and their mother was clearing the table for a meal. 'Supper's nearly ready!' she shouted to Arthur and Luke who were playing in the passage outside the kitchen. 'Boys, will you go and find Gwinnie, please.'

Arthur and Luke ran upstairs to Gwinnie's bedroom, but she wasn't there. 'Gwinnie, where are you?' they shouted. 'Come on, it's spaghetti Bolognese!'

They searched their own rooms and the bathroom, but she wasn't there either.

'Gwinnie! Gwinnie – ah, there you!' said
Luke as they rounded the door of their
mother's bedroom.

'Hi,' said Gwinnie. 'What do you think?' She
was kneeling on the floor, holding up her arm.
There were a lot of silver bangles jangling on
her wrist. A drawer of their mother's dressing
table was hanging open and there was a large
jewellery box on the floor.

'What are you doing?' said Arthur. 'You
can't just take Mum's jewellery.'

'It's OK. She lets me try on the stuff in this
box if I promise to put it back. It's not
precious. It's called costume jewellery,' said
Gwinnie, pleased that this was something that
she knew more about than her brothers.

Gwinnie smiled and held out her dress for
them to admire. But the boys had other ideas.

'What else has she got in there?' asked Luke.
'Hey, why don't we look in those other boxes?

I bet they're full of jewels!'

'We're not allowed to play with those,' said Gwinnie.

'Oh, come on, Gwinnie,' said Luke, getting on to his knees. 'We're not going to play with them. We're only going to have a look. Mum wouldn't mind. We'll put them back, so she won't even know.'

Gwinnie thought for a moment. 'OK,' she said. 'We'll just look.'

Slowly, the three children began to open the
boxes inside their mother's dressing table. They
found earrings, necklaces, chains and bracelets.
Some were bright and colourful; others were
small and delicate. Then, right at the back of
one of the drawers, Arthur found a small box
that looked different from the rest. It was
made of red leather and it had a gold pattern
engraved around the edges.

'Wow! Look at this one!' he said. 'This
looks precious.'

'What's inside?' asked Luke.

'Let's find out,' Arthur replied. He pulled at
the lid but it wouldn't open. 'It must be
locked,' he said, noticing the small keyhole at
the front.

'I bet it's got something pretty special
inside,' said Luke. 'Do you know where the key
is, Gwinnie?'

'No,' said Gwinnie. 'The only key I know

about is this one.' She walked over to her mother's bedside table and took a tiny gold key out from a pretty china pot. 'I found it one day when I was playing with Mum's jewellery, but Mum wouldn't tell me what it was for. She was a bit funny about it. "The key to my heart," she called it. She asked me never to touch it again so I haven't.'

'Let's see if it fits,' said Luke, taking it from his sister's hand. He wiggled the key into the tiny keyhole of the box and began to turn it. 'It works!' he said. He turned the key right round and, slowly, he opened the lid of the red leather box.

Inside, the children saw a long, delicate gold chain. On the end of the chain was a gold heart-shaped pendant with a beautiful diamond in the middle. The children recognized it immediately.

'Of course!' said Arthur. 'Mum's heart! The

key to her heart!'

This was their mother's favourite, and most precious, piece of jewellery. It had been given to her by the children's father just before he died. Their mother didn't talk about him so much any more. He had been killed in a climbing accident only a few months after Gwinnie had been born. Arthur had some distant memories of him but, to the others, old photographs were all they had to remind them of his place in the family. The children often wondered what he was like.

'What's that?' said Arthur, taking the box. Tucked up inside the lid was an old piece of folded paper. Arthur took it out, unfolded it and began to read.

'"*My darling,*
A small token of my love for you.
I wish I could give you more.

There is word in Camelot of treasure more
valuable than any that has ever been found
before.

If anyone is worthy of it, you are.

Whenever I go with Merlin, let this heart
remind you that my heart remains with you and
always will.

I love you.

Your devoted husband."'

'Her devoted husband!' gasped Luke in astonishment. 'That's our father!'

'Camelot! Treasure! Merlin!' stammered Arthur. 'What was he . . .? Why was he . . .? Could he have been . . .? No, it can't be true!'

Suddenly, the children looked up. They could hear footsteps right outside the room.

'Boys? Gwinnie? Where are you? Supper's ready.' It was their mother's voice.

Before the children could do anything, she was there in her bedroom, looking down at them as they sat on the floor, surrounded by the open boxes of her jewellery.

'Children, what are you doing?' she said. Her voice sounded anxious and alarmed. Then she saw the little red leather box and the letter in Arthur's hand. 'Arthur, give me that letter,' she said.

Arthur was too stunned to move. He looked up at his mother and he could see the worry and confusion in her eyes. 'I'm sorry, Mum,' said Arthur. 'We've read it. We couldn't help it.'

Arthur, Luke and Gwinnie all watched their mother's face as, slowly, her expression broke and tears began to fill her eyes. 'Oh, Arthur,' she said, her voice cracking. 'Oh, children . . . I've been meaning to tell you, but I just didn't know how. I thought maybe when you were a bit older . . . it's just so hard to understand . . .'

She stopped talking and sat down on the bed. Then she looked at Arthur, Luke and Gwinnie and took a long, deep breath. 'There's something I need to tell you about your father,' she said.

2. A Strange Revelation

'Your father was a great man,' said the children's mother. 'An adventurer. I've always told you that he was killed in a climbing accident in the mountains but . . . well . . . it's not true. The truth is much stranger than that.'

Arthur, Luke and Gwinnie sat down on the bed now, close to their mother. 'Sometimes,' she began, 'people who have very special qualities must fight bigger fights than those we have in our ordinary world. Your father was one of those people.'

She hugged her children. They drew closer and held her too. They could see that what she was about to say next was very important indeed.

'He was so strong, your father,' their mother continued. She took another deep breath. 'And that is why Merlin came for him.'

Luke, Arthur and Gwinnie glanced at each other, wide-eyed with astonishment.

'Yes,' said their mother, 'there *is* a real Merlin. Or at least there was. And Merlin led your father into another world – a world of knights and castles. He used to go to this other world, this world of Camelot, to help Merlin.'

'Our father was a *knight*?' said Arthur.

'Yes,' said their mother. 'I know it's hard to believe, but it's true. Evil forces were always at work in Camelot and your father was the one knight – strong and true, Merlin said – who he could rely on to do the right thing.'

She smiled, sadly yet proudly, at her children. 'And when I see you playing your own knights' games you remind me of him so much. You are all so like him in your own ways.'

Gwinnie squeezed her mother's hand. Arthur looked at Luke who was still taking in this incredible news. His mind was racing and he could see that Luke's was too.

'But one day,' continued their mother, 'one day he went with Merlin and . . . something terrible happened . . . he never returned. But Merlin made me a promise. He promised me that one day, however long it took, he would find a knight who would be strong and true enough to bring him back. And that I must never give up hope. Never stop believing that he would.'

Their mother's words tailed off and tears misted her eyes again. Arthur put his arms

round her and hugged her.

Luke hadn't seen his mother this upset before, but he knew that if he began to cry it would upset her even more. He would have to be strong; show her how brave he could be. He thought about the extraordinary things she had told them. Their father was a knight! He had gone with Merlin to Camelot! Could it be the same Camelot, the very same world that *they* had been to on their last adventure?

Their mother sniffed and began to speak again. 'I haven't seen Merlin since then,' she said. 'And the truth is, children, that I have given up hope. It's been such a long time. He was a wonderful man, your father. He loved you . . . he loved us all so much . . . and I'm never going to see him again.'

'But, Mum,' said Luke, 'we've been to —'

Arthur jabbed Luke sharply in the ribs and scowled at him.

'What?' said Luke.

Arthur grabbed Luke's hand and led him out of the bedroom into the passageway.

'We should tell her,' said Luke. '*We* can go to Camelot. We can look for our father. We can bring him back!'

'Do you think if we told her,' said Arthur, 'she'd let us go? She's lost her husband already. She'd never risk losing her children as well. We mustn't tell her we've been to Camelot. We mustn't tell her about Merlin, Luke. Not now.'

3. A Midnight Feast

'Mum,' said Gwinnie after supper, 'can I sleep in Luke's room tonight?'

'Good idea,' said the children's mother, worried that her tears might have upset them all. 'Why don't you all sleep in there tonight? You never know – there might even be a midnight feast!'

'Yeah! Midnight feast!' shouted Arthur, Luke and Gwinnie together.

'Teeth and pyjamas, then,' said their mum, smiling. 'I'll be up in a minute!'

The children raced upstairs, flung off their clothes, pulled on their pyjamas and cleaned their teeth. In no time, they were all tucked into the bunks in Luke's room, waiting eagerly for their mother to come upstairs with supplies.

As she kissed each of them goodnight, she left a little bag on their pillow. 'I love you all,' she said, turning off the light. 'You are wonderful children. You make me very proud.'

As soon as he heard his mother's footsteps fade away downstairs, Luke switched on the bedside light and the children leapt out of bed and sat together on the floor to eat the sweets in their bags. There were mini fried eggs, gums, shrimps, flying saucers – and fizzy cola bottles, Luke's absolute favourite.

'So our dad was a knight too,' said Arthur. 'And Merlin came for him, just like he came for us!'

'I can't believe it!' said Gwinnie. 'But it's true. Mum said!'

'I wonder if he was as brave as you were, Gwinnie,' said Arthur. 'When you rescued me and killed the dragon, Mandrake. When you threw that sword right through his neck!'

'What about me?' said Luke.

'Luke,' said Arthur, 'nobody is braver than you. If you hadn't gone after that evil witch Morgana, I wouldn't even be alive today. You saved my life, Luke. I'll never forget that.'

'What was the terrible thing that happened to our dad?' asked Gwinnie. 'Do you think he could still be there in Camelot? Do you think he could still be alive?'

'I don't know,' answered Luke, getting to his feet, 'but I'm going to find out.' He strode over to the door of his bedroom and gave the handle a sharp pull. The door opened and Luke looked out. All he could see was the boring yellow passageway.

'It doesn't work,' said Luke. 'When Merlin was here it opened like a drawbridge. There were fields and trees outside. It led all the way to Camelot. Why doesn't it work now?' He slammed the door in frustration.

'Maybe it only works when Merlin's here,' said Arthur. 'Anyway, Luke, we mustn't go. You saw how upset Mum was. Imagine if she came in tomorrow and we just . . . weren't here. We can't do that to her. We can't.'

The children climbed back into bed. 'The one knight Merlin really trusted,' Luke said. 'Strong and true. He must have been amazing, our dad. But what happened to him? Why couldn't he come back?'

'If only he could. It would make Mum so happy,' sighed Gwinnie.

'We must trust Merlin,' said Arthur.

'Remember what else he said. He would find a knight strong and true enough to bring our dad back.' He paused. 'But I wonder who?'

4. MERLIN

Luke awoke first. It was early and still too dark
to be morning, but there was a faint light
falling through the gap in his curtains.

He looked over at his clock and froze with
shock. 'Merlin!' he said.

'Hello, Luke,' said the figure standing tall
and still in the corner of Luke's room. He was
wearing a long, dark purple cloak and a black
silk skullcap. His twinkling eyes shone out
from his wrinkled face and a long white beard
grew from his chin.

'Merlin, you're here! You've come for us again, haven't you?' cried Luke, springing up with excitement. Last time Merlin had led Luke to Camelot, where Luke had recovered the Golden Shield and become a knight himself.

Now Arthur and Gwinnie were awake too, and as astonished as Luke was to see Merlin there.

'I have come for all of you,' Merlin said. 'We have trouble at Camelot. There is no time to lose!' He walked towards the door of Luke's bedroom.

'But, Merlin,' began Arthur. 'Our mother . . . we can't leave her. She's told us about our father . . . She's so upset. She needs us here.'

'What did she tell you about your father?' asked Merlin, fixing Arthur with his curious, sparkling eyes.

'That he was a knight too. That you needed

him in Camelot. That something terrible happened. And . . .' Arthur paused. 'That he's not coming back.'

'Your mother has stopped believing in her dreams,' said Merlin. 'Have you stopped believing in yours, Arthur?'

'But she'll be desperate if she finds out we're missing,' said Arthur. 'It's nearly morning. She'll be awake soon.'

'Don't worry,' said Merlin. 'Remember, time moves at a very different pace in my world. Very different indeed.'

'Is it true about our father?' asked Luke. 'Was he really a knight?'

Merlin nodded.

'What happened to him?' said Gwinnie. 'Why can't he come back?'

'So many questions!' said Merlin. 'All will be revealed in good time. Come, we must hurry. Luke, the door please.'

Luke turned the handle of his bedroom door
– and just like the last time Merlin came, it
creaked and began to lower from the top on
chains, like an old-fashioned drawbridge.

'I'm going,' Luke said to Arthur.

'Me too,' said Gwinnie.

Arthur stood by the doorway. 'It's all right,'
said Merlin. 'I understand how you feel. Trust
me, Arthur. Your family has long been my
closest concern.'

There was something in Merlin's eyes that

made Arthur believe him. Reluctantly, he
followed his brother and sister over the
drawbridge. In front of them, once more, was
not the yellow passageway – but a vast green
meadow with hills and valleys melting away
into the distance.

'Look, Luke,' shouted Gwinnie, in delight.
'It's Avalon!' She was pointing to a beautiful
white horse grazing beneath a large oak tree.

Avalon had been given to Luke by Merlin on
their last adventure. He recognized the
children immediately, and came trotting over.
Luke put his arm round Avalon's neck and
patted him. 'Avalon!' he said, beaming from
ear to ear. 'My good old friend, Avalon.'

Merlin had brought clothes in the saddlebags.
Arthur, Luke and Gwinnie changed into them,
then they all climbed on to Avalon's back.

As they rode, Merlin began to speak. 'A lot
has changed since you were last at Camelot,'

he said. 'Many of the children, some of whom are among the bravest of my knights, arc now missing.'

'Missing?' said Luke. 'Why?'

'The knights have heard a story that is leading them away from the safety of the castle,' said Mcrlin. 'They have heard that there is a magical hoard of treasure, amassed by the ancient kings of England. The Treasure of the Kings, they call it.'

'Is the story true?' asked Luke.

'It is,' Merlin replied.

Arthur and Gwinnie glanced at each other, both thinking the same thing. Could this be the treasure that their father talked about in his letter; the letter Arthur found with their mother's precious necklace?

'There were many items of this treasure,' Merlin continued, 'any one of which, even the smallest stone, would now be worth untold riches. Some of these treasures had magical powers but the most magical of them all was a belt. Pendragon's Belt. This belt gave its wearer everlasting life.'

'It must be the same treasure,' whispered Luke to Arthur. 'Dad said in his letter how valuable it was.'

'Shhh,' whispered Arthur. 'I know.'

'It is my belief that the knights are going in search of this treasure,' said Merlin. 'But they spare no thought for the terrible dangers that await them there; dangers beyond anything they have ever known before.'

Merlin looked at the children gravely. 'I will see you at Camelot,' he said. Then, instantly, he vanished.

'The Treasure of the Kings,' said Gwinnie. 'Wow!'

'Let's go!' said Luke. 'Come on, Avalon. Can you still fly?'

Avalon whinnied, broke into a gallop and then, whoosh! His mighty wings spread and they were climbing through the bright morning sky. Faster and higher they soared until, in the distance, Luke could see the familiar turrets, towers and battlements – of Camelot!

5. A FRIEND'S WARNING

Avalon landed gracefully at the gates of the castle. Merlin was there to greet them. 'Welcome!' he said. 'Your places await you.'

Arthur, Luke and Gwinnie left Avalon with a groom at the gates and walked through the courtyard into the Great Hall of Camelot.

The Round Table stood majestic at the end of the room. Around the table sat several boys dressed in their knights' armour, as well as a number of girls in fine costumes and jewellery. Luke recognized most of them. There was

Gawain, and Rufus. And beside Rufus, Luke saw the face of a dear old friend.

'Percival!' he shouted.

A boy of Luke's own age with red hair and freckles turned round. 'Luke? Luke! Is it really you?' he said, getting up from the table and running towards Luke. 'It is you! Sir Luke Lancelot! Welcome! And Sir Arthur and Lady Gwinnie too!'

Luke was overjoyed to see his old friend. 'Percival!' he said. 'You're sitting at the Round Table!'

'I'm a knight now too!' Percival replied. 'Come on! Sit down. Join us, all of you. It's so wonderful to see you!'

Luke, Arthur and Gwinnie greeted the other knights and ladies, and took their old places at the Round Table.

Morgana and Mandrake's seats remained empty. A reminder to all the knights of the last

great adventure; the recovery of the Golden Shield. The shield itself shone above them, high on the wall behind the Round Table.

Luke noticed that a number of the other seats round the table were now empty as well. 'Is it true what Merlin told us?' Luke asked Percival. 'That a lot of the knights have gone missing? That they've gone in search of treasure more beautiful than any that has been known before?'

Percival lowered his eyes and stared at the table. 'It is true,' he said.

Luke felt sure Percival was hiding something from him. 'Percival,' he said, 'what do you know about this? What has been happening?'

'I can't tell you anything more, Luke,' said Percival, still looking away. 'It's too dangerous.'

'Why?' asked Luke. 'What is so dangerous?'

'Luke, please, I can't tell you,' said Percival. 'It's more than my life is worth.' He looked up

at Luke, real fear in his eyes. 'I'm so glad
you're here,' he said. 'Maybe you can help us.'
His voice began to quiver. 'Oh, I hope you can.'

6. Pendragon's Belt

'Luke, Arthur, Gwinnie,' said Merlin. 'Come with me. I have something to show you.'

The children got up from the Round Table and followed Merlin through the castle until they came to a large oak door at the end of a passageway.

'This is my study,' Merlin told them.

Inside the room were a great many books of all shapes and sizes. Some were arranged neatly on shelves; others sat in huge piles around a wide desk. Merlin walked over to the

fireplace, beside which was a large, silver
candlestick sunk into the wall. He grasped the
candlestick and pulled it towards him.

A grating sound came from the wall above
the fireplace. The children watched in
astonishment as one of the stones in the
middle of the wall revolved to reveal a big iron
key, which hung on a hook on the other side of
the stone.

'Wow!' said Luke. 'A secret cupboard!'

'Indeed,' said Merlin. 'But you must tell no

one about this. None of you. You never know
who you can trust.'

Merlin took the key and went over to a wide
stone panel that was set into the wall behind
his desk. He put the iron key into a keyhole
and turned it. He raised the panel and looked
at Luke, Arthur and Gwinnie. 'Pendragon's
Belt,' he said.

'Pendragon's Belt!' exclaimed Luke. 'From
the Treasure of the Kings? The belt that gives
its wearer everlasting life?'

'Exactly,' said Merlin.

The children stared, open-mouthed.

'It's beautiful,' said Gwinnie.

'Amazing,' said Arthur.

'The treasure passed through many
generations of the Pendragon line,' continued
Merlin, 'until it came to King Uther. Uther
was a wise king. He saw that treasure brought
nothing but greed and that greed brought

nothing but violence. So he hid the treasure in a secret place. Furthermore, he got a sorcerer to cast a spell on it. There is an inscription carved on a stone tablet beside the treasure, warning anyone who dares try to take it of what will happen to them.'

'What does it say?' asked Luke.

'This,' said Merlin . . .

"If to stone you won't be turned
Heed well what I have taught:
He who takes the treasure
Must be pure in deed and thought."'

'What does that mean?' asked Luke.

'No one can take the treasure without being turned to stone unless their thoughts are pure,' replied Merlin. 'But it's hard to keep your thoughts pure with treasure as valuable and as powerful as that. You think of all the things you could have in exchange for just one piece. You get greedy. It's just too tempting. But there's more . . .' Merlin continued.

'"But he who takes the belt complete
Will risk the mountain's ire,
For never shall it leave this place
Without a sea of fire."

'If anyone were to try to take Pendragon's Belt,' explained Merlin, 'then they would have

to face the mountain's ire – its anger.'

'But what kind of a mountain becomes angry?' Luke asked.

'A volcano?' suggested Gwinnie.

'Exactly,' Merlin replied. 'A volcano!'

7. THE MISSING JEWEL

Merlin began to pace around his study. 'Some time ago,' he said, 'a clue was found to the location of the treasure. I feared for the safety of my knights and for Camelot itself. So I sent my best knight, a knight who was strong and true, a knight with the purest heart I have known, to fetch the belt and bring it back here to safety where I could watch over it.

'However,' continued Merlin, 'do you see that hole at the front of the belt?'

The children looked. There were jewels all

the way round the belt, except at the very centre, where there was a buckle. In the middle of the buckle was a large hole.

'There was once a jewel there as well,' said Merlin. 'The largest jewel in the belt. I ordered the knight to remove this jewel and to leave it with the rest of the treasure, then go back for it later. That way, the belt would not be "complete" and the spell would not work. He brought back the belt and went back for the jewel. That's when something went wrong.'

The children listened in silence, willing Merlin to go on.

'The knight I sent couldn't resist picking up one other piece of treasure,' Merlin continued. 'It was just a small gold brooch, but that was enough. His thoughts, his deeds, were no longer pure. He was stealing. And when he turned to bring the jewel back to Camelot –' Merlin stopped and fixed his gaze on Luke,

Arthur and Gwinnie – 'he turned to stone.
Solid stone, with the brooch in one hand and
the belt's jewel clasped tightly in the other.'

'Who was that knight?' asked Luke.

Merlin put a hand on Luke's shoulder and
gathered Arthur and Gwinnie towards him as
well. 'That knight, children . . .' he said, 'was
your father.'

Luke's mouth fell open. He gasped.

Arthur closed his eyes and covered his face

with his hands. His father was a distant memory, but out of all the children, it was he who remembered him the best.

Gwinnie reached for Arthur's hand.

'I don't understand,' said Luke. 'Is he still alive?'

Oh, Luke,' sighed Merlin, 'that is a hard question to answer. And none of my knights – your friends – bring news of him. All, it seems, have been too tempted by the treasure to be able to return.'

'Why are they going after the treasure again?' asked Gwinnie. 'How do they know about it?'

'I do not know,' replied Merlin, 'but I suspect that evil forces are at work. Somehow, my knights of the Round Table have discovered the location of the treasure again and they are trying to steal it. Perhaps it is simply the lure of the treasure itself; perhaps it is something more sinister.'

Merlin sighed and looked at the children. 'Sometimes the most beautiful things are the most dangerous,' he said. 'Greed is a terrible thing; it can distort even the purest of minds. After all, it is not always what we *have* that makes us happy.'

With these words, Merlin reached up towards the belt and closed the stone panel over it. He locked it with the key, which he put back on its hook in the secret cupboard. When Merlin raised the candlestick beside the fireplace, the cupboard door revolved and closed. The wall was just a wall again.

'I am sorry,' said Merlin, looking at Luke, Arthur and Gwinnie once more. 'Your father was a great knight.'

'But you said you'd find someone who could bring him back,' said Arthur. 'You told our mother.'

'I did,' replied Merlin, 'and I will.' Then he

walked out of the room.

'Merlin!' shouted Luke, running out after him. 'Wait! Who are you going to find to do this? Who is going to bring him back?'

Merlin turned round. He looked straight into Luke's puzzled eyes, as if searching for something behind them. Then his face broke into a smile, he nodded at Luke with a twinkle in his eye and, suddenly, he was gone.

Arthur and Gwinnie joined Luke. 'Where's Merlin?' said Gwinnie.

'I don't know,' said Luke. 'He disappeared.'

'What did he say?' Arthur asked.

'He didn't say anything. He just looked at me. It was as if he was looking into my mind . . . as if he was asking me to do something.'

Luke thought for a moment then spoke again. 'We must go and find him,' he said. 'We must go and find our father.'

'But we don't know where he is,' said

Arthur. 'Even if we did, you heard what Merlin said. Surely he wouldn't want us to go. It's too dangerous.'

'And if we went,' said Gwinnie, 'even if we found him – he's been turned to stone. How would we turn him back? Merlin doesn't even seem sure he's still alive.'

8. A SECRET PLAN

Luke, Arthur and Gwinnie returned to the
Great Hall and sat down at the Round Table,
their minds racing with the extraordinary
secrets that Merlin had just revealed to them.

'A belt that brings you everlasting life,' said
Arthur. 'And we've seen it! Think how much
Morgana would have liked to get her hands on
that. The Golden Shield would have made her
invincible, but everlasting life . . .!' Luke and
Gwinnie smiled, thankful that the old sorceress
was dead and would no longer be able to bring

trouble to Camelot.

'What about that amazing stone panel!' said
Luke. 'And the candlestick, and the secret
cupboard with the key!'

'The key?' said a voice behind them. It was
Percival. Hastily, he sat down beside Luke. 'You
know where the key is?' He was leaning very
close to Luke, staring at him with an urgent,
almost desperate look in his eyes.

'Merlin told us not to tell anyone,' said Luke.

'Then I suppose you don't want to know where the clue is to the location of the treasure.' Percival was whispering now. 'I suppose you don't want to find your father.'

Luke grabbed him by the arm. 'What do you know about our father?' he barked.

'I know that he's been turned to stone,' Percival replied. Luke could tell that Percival knew more than he was letting on. And he could see from his eyes that he was frightened – very frightened indeed.

'Who told you?' asked Luke. 'How do you know?'

'I can't tell you,' said Percival. 'They'll kill me. You're too close to Merlin. They say that if Merlin finds out, we'll all be dead.'

'Calm down,' said Gwinnie, and Luke let go of Percival's arm. 'We'll tell you where the key

57

is,' Gwinnie went on, 'if you help us to find the clue to the treasure.'

'OK,' said Percival. 'I'll help you. Meet me at the top of the cellar stairs tonight after Merlin has gone to bed.'

9. THE HIDDEN CLUE

Luke waited until he heard the door of
Merlin's bedchamber close. Then he crept into
the passageway and listened until he could hear
snoring.

Slowly, he tiptoed into Arthur's bedchamber
and then Gwinnie's, waking them up and
leading them out to the top of the huge stone
staircase of Camelot. Silently, the three of
them crept down the stairs.

Aside from a thin crescent of moon, which
shone a dim, ghostly light through the

windows of the castle, everything was dark. At the top of the stairs which led down to the cellars they hid in the shadows, waiting for Percival.

'Where is he?' whispered Arthur. 'He must have changed his mind. I knew we shouldn't be doing this.'

'Shhh,' said Luke. 'I think I can see something.'

A dim point of light had appeared at the far end of the passage. It came towards them and it wasn't long before the children recognized Percival, carrying a flaming torch in front of him.

'Good,' said Luke. 'You came. So – where is the clue?'

'Well, I don't know where it is exactly,' said Percival, 'but I do know that it's carved on a wall.'

'What wall?' asked Luke. 'Where?'

'A wall right here,' said Percival, 'at the

bottom of the castle of Camelot itself. It's somewhere down in the cellars.'

'But we're not allowed down there,' said Arthur.

'If we all stick together we'll be all right,' said Luke. 'If we don't try to find the clue we're never going to find our father. Come on, follow me.'

Luke began to climb down the steep steps. Percival followed with his torch. Gwinnie and Arthur were close behind.

When they got to the bottom of the steps, the children stopped. There was a maze of dark archways and rooms leading off the passage in front of them. The light from Percival's flickering torch was casting moving shapes and shadows on to the walls, making it feel as though they were not alone.

'Let's look through the rooms one by one,' said Luke.

They began to walk through the first
archway, then Gwinnie felt something touch
her face. 'Aagh!' she screamed.

'It's only a cobweb,' said Luke.

'I hate spiders,' said Gwinnie, brushing the
remains of the web from her face. Luke took
her hand. 'Walk with me,' he said.

Suddenly, Arthur stopped still. 'Did you hear
that?' he whispered.

'What?' said Percival. He looked terrified.

'I think I heard a noise,' said Arthur. 'A kind of strange, distant roar.'

They all waited and listened, but heard nothing. 'Come on,' said Luke. 'Let's keep looking. We *must* find the clue.'

They searched on through room after room, but none of the walls had anything on them. They were just dark, cold stone.

'Are you sure it's down here, Percival?' said Arthur. 'I don't like this. It doesn't feel right. I think we should go back.'

'Wait,' said Gwinnie. 'What's this? Percival, bring your torch over here. I think I've found something!'

Percival raced over to Gwinnie who was brushing dust from the surface of a wall.

'It looks like an inscription,' said Arthur. He squinted his eyes and began to read.

'"You must cross the Lake of Souls
To find what you desire..."

'It is!' said Arthur. 'It is an inscription. This must be the clue!'

Gwinnie brushed more and, slowly, more letters began to reveal themselves.

Arthur began to read again.

' "You must cross the Lake of Souls
To find what you desire.
The Treasure of the Kings is hidden
In the Room of Fire." '

'It's the clue to the Treasure of the Kings!' shouted Luke, overjoyed. 'I knew we'd find it!'

'The Lake of Souls,' said Arthur. 'I know where that is! Merlin's told me about it before.'

'Where?' asked Gwinnie.

'It's beyond the forest outside the castle

gates,' Arthur replied. 'People say that strange
spirits haunt it. That's why it's called the Lake
of Souls. And that's why no one ever dares go
there,' he added slowly.

'Well,' said Percival, 'I kept my side of the
bargain. It's time for you to keep yours. Where
is the key?'

'Look, Percival,' said Arthur. 'It's one thing
leading us down into the cellars to look for
this clue, but I really don't think we should tell
you. Merlin told us not to let *anyone* –'

'Your father will die!' said Percival.
'Although he has been turned to stone, his
spirit is still alive, but not for long. They've got
a new plan. They're going to smash him to
pieces.'

'What?' said Arthur, hardly able to believe
what he was hearing.

'They're going to smash him to release the
jewel from his hand,' said Percival. 'The jewel

from Pendragon's Belt. And if they smash him, his spirit will die. It will no longer be able to return to his body. There will be no body to return to – just a million pieces of shattered stone and dust. But maybe if I get them the belt . . .'

'What are you talking about?' Arthur was shouting now. 'Who's going to smash him?'

'Hush!' said Percival. 'Quiet! It's not safe.' He looked around nervously, holding his torch out in front of him and squinting through the shadows.

'They come for us in the night,' whispered Percival. 'They make us try – one after another – to take bits of treasure. They say there must be a way to take it without being turned to stone. They say we must find it. They promise any knight who succeeds can keep his treasure. So some go willingly. But others . . .' Percival shivered. 'Others don't.' Percival's words tailed off into a whimper.

Luke set his hands on Percival's shoulders and looked into his eyes. 'Who's "they"?' he said. 'Who is doing this, Percival?'

'You won't believe me if I tell you, Luke,' said Percival. 'You won't believe it's possible.'

'Tell me!' Luke demanded. His voice was strong and deliberate.

Percival looked back at Luke. 'Morgana,' he said.

'Impossible!' snapped Luke. 'Morgana's dead.'

'That's what I thought,' said Percival. 'But she's not. And it's not just Morgana.'

'Mandrake?' said Gwinnie. 'Don't tell me Mandrake's still alive too. I drove my sword right into his neck. I watched him die!'

'No,' said Percival. 'Mandrake's dead all right. But Morgana has another brother – a dragonman. His name is Dragor.'

'What's a dragonman?' asked Arthur.

'Half man, half dragon,' said Percival. 'He's a terrifying beast. He's behind this. It's him who told the knights about the inscription. It's him who promises them they can keep their treasure. It's him who takes them away.'

Percival sighed. 'There. Now I've told you,' he said. 'But please, swear on your lives that you won't tell Merlin. If you tell Merlin they'll kill us all.'

Luke, Arthur and Gwinnie did as Percival asked.

'It's your turn now,' said Percival. 'Where's the key? I know there's a secret cupboard in Merlin's study. There must be a button . . . a lever . . .?'

'The candlestick,' said Luke.

At that moment, there was a loud, rasping roar. The children jumped. Luke's heart began to thump wildly. 'Quick!' he said. 'Behind this wall!'

Arthur, Luke and Gwinnie pressed themselves up behind a cold, stone archway.

Percival blew out the flame of his torch. They were in total darkness.

Soon the children could hear slow, heavy footsteps. They were getting closer. Then suddenly, 'Roooaarrr!' A huge burst of flame lit up the passageway.

For a moment, Arthur, Luke and Gwinnie could see each other's terrified faces. They huddled together, tight against the wall, silent except for the heavy beating of their hearts. Then the footsteps began again. They were walking away. The children kept absolutely still until they were gone.

'Phew,' said Arthur, stepping out from behind the archway. 'That was close!'

'Was that him, Percival?' said Gwinnie. 'That awful roar . . . and the flames . . . was that the dragonman?'

But Percival did not reply.

'Percival!' shouted Arthur through the darkness. 'Percival, where are you?'

Still there was no reply.

'He's gone!' said Luke.

'Quick!' cried Gwinnie. 'The key . . . the belt!'

As quickly as they could, Arthur, Luke and Gwinnie found their way back to the entrance to the cellars. They raced up the stairs, where the first light of dawn was beginning to show, and ran along the passageway into Merlin's study.

Luke pulled the candlestick beside the fireplace. The stone revolved. The key was gone.

'The panel, Arthur,' he said. But Arthur was already there. The panel was unlocked and when Arthur lifted the lid, he, Luke and Gwinnie could all see that there was nothing behind it at all.

Pendragon's Belt had gone.

10. A Difficult Decision

'What have we done?' said Arthur. 'The belt has gone! What will Merlin say? I knew we should never have got into this. We should have stayed at home. What do we do now?'

Suddenly, the door opened. Arthur, Luke and Gwinnie stepped back in horror as Merlin appeared.

'Merlin,' began Arthur, 'I'm so sorry. We didn't know what to do . . . we thought that maybe . . .'

Merlin raised his hand to stop Arthur from

talking. He looked in silence at the open stone panel and the place where the belt used to be.

'It is difficult, isn't it?' he said. To Arthur's surprise, Merlin didn't look angry at all. Instead, his eyes were warm and understanding, and his voice was deep and calm.

'You are wise, Arthur,' said Merlin. 'Wise beyond your years. One day you will make a great king. But sometimes there are decisions to be made that no amount of wisdom or learning can prepare you for. These are the hardest decisions of all. When you are faced with them, there is only one thing to do.'

Merlin put his arm round Arthur's shoulder. 'Follow your heart, Arthur,' he said. 'Do what your heart tells you to do and you will never be wrong.'

Arthur listened in silence to Merlin's words. As he stood there, a strange feeling of certainty came over him. He realized what Merlin was saying. He had wanted to stay to look after his mother – that was true – but now they were here in Camelot. They had discovered that his father could still be alive and that his life was in terrible danger. What could they do now but try to rescue him?

However dangerous it might be, Arthur knew that there was only one thing to do. They had to find the treasure. They had to try to save their father's life.

'You see?' said Merlin, smiling as he watched Arthur with twinkling eyes. 'When you listen to your heart it's easy. But your heart doesn't always tell you the easiest thing to do.'

11. THE FOREST OF ENDLESS NIGHT

'To the armoury!' said Arthur. 'We've got no time to lose.'

With Luke and Gwinnie following close behind, Arthur marched back down the passageway outside Merlin's study, through the Great Hall, and into another corridor, at the end of which was a wooden door with wide metal hinges.

Inside the room were rows and rows of suits of armour and racks of shields and swords. Luke found the silver shield that Merlin had

given him on his last visit to Camelot,
embossed with his knight's initials, LL, for
Luke Lancelot, in gold, and he picked out his
precious jewelled sword. He strapped on his
gleaming breastplate and grabbed his weapon.

Arthur did the same. 'Here, Gwinnie,' he
said. 'You should take some armour, and this
sword.' He found a small chain-mail coat,
which he handed to Gwinnie, and a light, sharp
sword, which she buckled round her waist.

'Come on,' he said. 'Let's go!'

Arthur, Luke and Gwinnie ran together out into the courtyard of Camelot.

'Avalon!' shouted Luke.

Avalon came cantering towards him. Luke, Arthur and Gwinnie all leapt on to his back.

'Fly, Avalon,' commanded Luke. 'Fly!'

Avalon needed no further urging. He broke into a gallop and, just before they reached the castle gates, he stretched his mighty wings and soared up into the clear morning air, over the gates and out above the castle grounds.

'The Lake of Souls?' Luke shouted back to Arthur. 'Where is it?'

'We need to fly over that forest there,' said Arthur, pointing towards a vast, dark mass of trees that seemed to stretch out as far as the horizon. 'It's beyond it on the other side.'

Luke steered Avalon towards the forest. The sun was still rising in the sky, but the air around them appeared to be getting thicker and darker. 'What's happening?' said Gwinnie. 'I thought it was still morning.'

'The forest is a strange place,' said Arthur. 'Dark magic rules here. Some people call it the Forest of Endless Night. It's not like the world of Camelot. Merlin said witches make their homes in these trees. That's why nobody comes here.' He held his sister tightly round the waist. 'We'll look after you,' he said.

'We'll all look after each other,' Gwinnie shouted back to him bravely.

12. The Lake of Souls

As Avalon flew further, Luke, Arthur and Gwinnie began to make out the far edge of the forest and, beyond that, a still, black stretch of water. The sun had completely disappeared now. In its place was a soft moon, half hidden by clouds. The moon on the water made it gleam like a slab of pale silver, rippled with ink.

'The Lake of Souls,' announced Arthur with a shiver.

Suddenly, Avalon whinnied and threw his

head from side to side. His wings seemed to lose their grip on the air and they began to fall, out of control, towards the edge of the water.

'Avalon!' shouted Luke. 'What's happening? Help!'

But Avalon was falling fast, twisting and flailing with his hooves.

'Go back!' shouted Gwinnie. 'Steer him back, Luke!'

Luke pulled hard on the reins and managed to get Avalon to turn his head away from the lake and back towards the forest.

The ground was hurtling towards them but – just as they were about to slam into the trees – Avalon beat his wings, swooped steeply away from the edge of the forest and landed softly on the ground beside the lake.

'Wow!' said Luke, panting hard as he dismounted. 'That was close! Gwinnie, you

saved our lives! How did you know to turn
back?'

'When we found the clue in the cellars at
Camelot, Arthur, you said you thought that the
lake was haunted. Well, I read in a book once
that you can't fly over a haunted place; nothing
can. Not even Avalon!'

Luke patted Avalon on the neck and stroked
his cheek. 'There, there,' he said. 'It's all right.
We understand. Thank you, Avalon. You've got
us this far. We can go the rest of the way on
our own. You've done more than enough. You

stay here and wait for us to return.'

Luke, Arthur and Gwinnie walked to the edge of the lake. A low, thick mist hung just above the surface of the water.

'What's this?' said Arthur. 'Look.' Hidden in some reeds was a long, narrow boat. The children stepped into it and found two oars in the bottom.

'I'll row,' said Luke. 'You two keep a lookout and tell me where we're going.'

They pushed the boat out into the lake and, almost at once, were enveloped in the mist. 'I can't see anything,' said Arthur from the front. But Luke rowed on and, after a while, the mist cleared a little and their eyes became more used to the eerie darkness.

Suddenly, Gwinnie screamed. A huge, pale, ghostly face was right in front of her.

'HEEELLLP!' it shrieked, wailing from the hole where its mouth would have been were it

human. Just as suddenly, the face disappeared again into the mist.

'Gwinnie,' said Luke, letting go of his oars and holding her tightly. 'Are you OK?'

'Yes,' said Gwinnie, her heart racing. 'I'm fine. What was *that*?'

'It must have been some kind of spirit,' said Luke. 'You were right. This lake is definitely haunted.'

'Look,' said Arthur. 'Over there!'

Another ghostly figure was drifting over the water in front of them. And now they could see more of them, gliding like white, smoky shadows over the surface of the lake.

'I wonder who they are?' said Gwinnie. 'They look so sad.' It was true. Each hollow, empty face was twisted into a painful expression of despair. And the low, moaning wails the children heard could only be the cries of those who had lost all hope.

Suddenly, Arthur shouted out, 'Father!'

'What?' said Luke. 'What do you mean? Did you see him?'

'No,' said Arthur, 'I didn't see him, but I can feel him. He's near us; I know it. It felt as if he just brushed past me.' Arthur wrapped his arms over his chest and shivered. 'We're getting close,' he said.

'Look!' cried Gwinnie suddenly. 'I can see something. Over there!'

Luke and Arthur looked to where Gwinnie was pointing. In the distance, they saw the silhouette of a mountain rising up from an island in the middle of the lake.

'Look at the top,' said Gwinnie. A thin curl of dark smoke was rising up from the very centre of the mountain. 'It must be a volcano. Just like Merlin said!'

'Then the Room of Fire . . .' said Arthur slowly, 'must be the heart of the volcano itself!'

13. THE DRAGONMAN

The boat reached the shore of the island and Luke, Arthur and Gwinnie dragged it up to where several other boats lay half hidden in the reeds.

The volcano rose up in front of them, huge and dark against the moonlit sky. 'How do we get in?' said Luke. 'It's just thick, solid rock.'

Suddenly, there was a loud roar behind them. The children froze in fear. It was the very same roar that they had heard in the cellars at Camelot. Then again, 'Roooaaar!'

Luke turned. His heart pounded and his mouth fell open in a gasp of terrified surprise. Pacing towards them was a huge beast.

Luke had never seen anything like it before. From the bottom, it looked like a man, but larger than a man. However, from the waist up, its bare chest began to turn green and scaly. Its arms were as thick as small trees, and at the ends of its enormous hands were sharp, craggy claws.

Fire was flaring from its wide nostrils and, in the light of the flames, Luke could see its giant jaws, its long, sharp teeth and its yellow eyes. This could only be the head of a dragon.

'The dragonman!' gasped Arthur. 'It must be the dragonman that Percival told us about. Dragor!'

'What are you children doing here?' roared the dragonman. In one of his hands was a long, heavy sword. In the other was a huge spiked

metal ball swinging from a chain – a mace.

'We have come to rescue our father!'
shouted Gwinnie.

Dragor fixed her with his shining yellow
eyes. 'You killed my brother,' he said, his voice
full of menace, 'and now I'm going to get my
revenge!'

Dragor hurled his mace to the ground and
pounded towards Gwinnie with his huge sword
outstretched. Arthur, Luke and Gwinnie all
drew their weapons, ready to fight back.

Now Dragor was towering over Gwinnie.

Flames were bursting from his jaws. His sword was slashing through the air. *Slash! Swoosh! Crash!*

Gwinnie's sword was small and light, and no match for Dragor's powerful blows, but she was fast and managed to dance out of the way of the thrashing blade.

Then she lunged at his stomach and her sword caught the soft skin of his belly.

'Aaagh!' roared Dragor, looking down at the deep gash. He grasped it with his scaly hand as the dark blood began to ooze, hardly able to believe that such a small enemy could have inflicted such a wound.

Then he looked up at Gwinnie with vicious narrowed eyes, raised his sword above his head and slammed it down towards her. Gwinnie leapt out of the way, darted behind him and drove her sword into his back.

Dragor roared again and spun round to face her. He pulled out Gwinnie's sword, wincing

with the pain and, with his eyes still fixed on
Gwinnie, he took it in both hands, bent the
blade double and threw it far away behind him.

'What have you got to defend yourself with
now, little girl?' roared Dragor, pacing towards
her with his sword.

'She's got *us*!' yelled Luke as he and Arthur
slashed at the dragonman with their sharp
blades. 'Run, Gwinnie! Find a way into the
mountain!'

'Roooaaar!' Dragor turned to face Luke.
There was fury in his eyes. He came stumbling
forwards and slammed his sword against Luke's
shield. The blow was so fierce that Luke was
sent hurtling to the ground. His arm was cut
and bleeding.

'Take this!' shouted Arthur, stepping
between Luke and Dragor and slashing at the
dragonman. Their swords met with a crash.
Again, Arthur swung his sword at Dragor – but

Dragor sliced back with such force that the
blade of Arthur's sword was shattered.

Arthur had nothing left but a dagger. And
now Dragor was right in front of him. 'This is
for my brother!' the dragonman roared,
wielding his sword with both hands high above
his head.

'Here!' shouted Luke, who was still on the
ground. 'Take my sword!' He flung it to Arthur
just in time for Arthur to deflect Dragor's
blow.

Arthur lunged back at Dragor, but Dragor parried the blow. On and on they fought, metal crashing against metal. Then, with a great swoosh, Dragor knocked Luke's sword from Arthur's hand. He pounced on it with his scaly claws, picked it up, and threw it with all his might towards the volcano behind them.

'Arthur! You've got to get it!' yelled Luke, picking himself up off the ground. 'It's the only sword we've got left! I'll be all right. Just hurry!'

Arthur ran towards the volcano to retrieve the sword.

Dragor came towards Luke, sword in hand. A great jet of flame belched from his mouth. It sent Luke reeling to the ground again. He could feel the scaring heat against his skin.

Dragor looked down at Luke with hate in his eyes. He raised his sword. Then . . . 'No,' he said, suddenly hesitating. 'Not the sword. I'll finish you off with my mace. Just like I'm going to finish off your father!'

'No!' yelled Luke. 'Arthur! Arthur, where are you? Help!'

But Arthur was nowhere to be seen.

Luke scrambled frantically across the ground, his arm hurt and bleeding, desperately trying to find his sword. Suddenly, he saw the jewels on its hilt glinting in the dust. His fingers closed round the handle. Then he felt a sharp tug on his leg – and he fell through a hole in the ground.

He landed with a thud, looking up just in time to see a grass-covered door close quickly above him.

Gwinnie was holding his ankle and Arthur was crouching beside them. 'Shhh!' whispered Gwinnie, holding a finger to her mouth. 'Not a sound!'

There was a roar above them. 'Where are you?' bellowed Dragor. 'I'm going to get you.

I'm going to get you all! I will find you in the mountain. I will hunt you down. You will never get away from here alive!'

Luke, Arthur and Gwinnie stayed absolutely still, with pounding hearts and sweating palms, until they could no longer hear Dragor's footsteps or angry roars.

14. Inside the Volcano

'Where are we?' said Luke, looking around. 'What happened?'

'I think it must be some sort of secret tunnel,' said Gwinnie. 'I knew we had to find a way to escape from Dragor, so I started looking for a way into the mountain, just like you said. Then I saw this patch of grass. It looked a bit different and when I stepped on it, it gave way. So I pulled Arthur in too, when I could, and then you.'

'Looks like you've saved us all again,

Gwinnie,' said Luke. 'Thank you.' He looked around. He could make out a series of passageways carved through the rock in front of them. They were lit by a dim, orange glow that seemed to get brighter as it got further away.

'What's that noise?' asked Gwinnie suddenly.

The children all listened. There it was again; a long, deep, low rumble.

'It sounds like it's coming from the heart of the volcano,' said Arthur.

'Which way do we go?' said Luke, his voice echoing eerily down the tunnel in front of them. 'There are so many passageways. It's like a maze.'

'Well,' said Gwinnie, 'if we're looking for the Room of Fire, surely we should walk towards where the light's coming from.'

'Good idea,' said Arthur. 'Let's go!'

Luke, Arthur and Gwinnie began to walk straight down the tunnel in front of them, deep into the volcano. The rumbling sound was getting louder and, as they walked, the air inside the tunnel was getting hotter.

'What's that?' said Arthur, pointing at a shape in the distance. It looked like the figure of a person, but it was standing absolutely still.

'Who is it?' Luke shouted down the tunnel.

But the figure didn't reply, or move.

They got closer. It was definitely a boy; a boy of about their own age and a knight as well.

'Who are you?' began Luke again. 'What . . .' and then he stopped in horror. Suddenly, he realized what it was he was looking at.

There, in front of them, with his face set in a horrified, twisted scream, a golden goblet in one hand and the other shielding his eyes as if he were running from something truly terrible, was the frozen figure of their old friend Percival – turned completely to stone.

15. A DEAD END

Suddenly, there was a ferocious roar behind them.

'Dragor!' said Gwinnie. 'He's found his way in!'

'Run!' shouted Arthur and he, Luke and Gwinnie began to race down the tunnel.

There were more and more passageways leading off in every direction. 'This way,' shouted Arthur. 'Follow me!'

They turned off the main tunnel and darted into a dark entrance. Almost at once, they

could see that it led nowhere. They were in a
tiny stone chamber: a dead end. 'What do we
do now?' said Gwinnie. 'We're trapped!'

'Sshhh!' whispered Arthur. 'Keep close to
the wall. Don't move.'

'Aaaah!' yelped Gwinnie, stumbling against a
strange shape in the darkness. 'There's
someone here!'

Luke clapped a hand over her mouth and drew
his sword. Nobody moved. The children could
all feel their hearts pounding inside their chests.

Dragor's footsteps were getting closer.
'Where are you?' he bellowed. 'I know you're
here somewhere.' Then he stopped.

'I can smell you,' he said, menacingly. He

was very close to their hiding place. The children desperately tried to hold their breath.

There was another deafening roar and a great burst of flame. It lit up the small stone chamber where the children were hiding. Now Luke and Arthur could see why Gwinnie had screamed. She had pressed herself up against another figure; another knight turned completely to stone. He had a gold crown in one hand and the same agonized scream on his face as Percival. It was Sir Rufus.

'When I find you,' roared Dragor, 'I'm going to burn you to cinders. Wouldn't Morgana be pleased about that!' He let out a rasping laugh.

The children glanced at one another, open-mouthed.

Then Dragor's footsteps began again. 'Daddy's going to feel my mace!' he roared, before walking away down the tunnel.

He had lost them – for the time being, at least.

16. THE ROOM OF FIRE

When they were sure that Dragor had gone,
Luke, Arthur and Gwinnie hurtled out of the
small stone chamber where they had been
hiding and ran back into the main tunnel.

'Morgana!' said Luke. 'So what Percival said
was true. But how can she still be alive?
Mandrake burnt her to death with his breath.'

'That's what I thought,' said Gwinnie.

'We must hurry!' cried Luke. 'You heard
what Dragor said about his mace. Percival was
right about that too. We can't let him destroy

our father. Come on!'

Arthur, Luke and Gwinnie scrambled on down the tunnel as fast as they could. As they went deeper into the mountain they began to see more knights: adults now, as well as children. And all of them were set solid in stone, with a treasure in one hand, and the other hand shielding their eyes. Like Percival and Rufus, their faces were all frozen in terrified screams.

'Look at them,' said Gwinnie with a shiver. 'What could they have been running from?'

'I don't know,' said Arthur. 'And I'm not sure I want to find out.'

The tunnel had got much hotter now. The orange glow was becoming brighter and the rumbling sound was getting louder.

'I think that's the end,' said Luke, pointing. 'Look!'

Slowly, they crept to the end of the tunnel. Then they stopped, mouths open. They couldn't believe what they were looking at.

In front of them was a huge, round chamber of stone. Around the edge of the chamber was a bank; a wide stone ledge with many tunnels, just like the one the children were in, leading away from the room back into the mountain. In front of the bank was a moat. But it was not just an ordinary moat. This moat was roaring and bubbling with red-hot lava.

'The Room of Fire!' said Gwinnie, wide-eyed with wonder.

Over the moat was a rickety rope bridge, with steps made of wooden planks, leading on to a small island. And in the middle of the island was a vast pile of treasure: jewellery, goblets, armour, dishes of gold and silver, and gems and precious stones of every shape, size and colour.

The treasure glowed and sparkled like nothing else the children had ever seen before. It felt like it had a mysterious and powerful magic to it.

'It's wonderful!' whispered Arthur, understanding for himself now why the knights had found it so hard to resist the temptation of these strange and beautiful objects.

Beside the treasure was a figure pacing up and down with small, anxious steps. Despite the hood covering her face, Luke, Arthur and

Gwinnie all recognized her at once. Draped in
a black cloak, her bony frame hunched and
bent as she walked, was the unmistakable
shape of their old enemy. Morgana.

Beside Morgana stood the stone figure of
another knight: a man. He was tall and
imposing. Like the other stone knights, his face
was turned away from the treasure but, unlike
them, it looked calm and strong, as though he
was resigned to his fate with dignity and
courage.

In one of his hands was a small, gold brooch. In the other, with his fingers clasped tightly round it, was a large, bright, sparkling jewel.

'Father!' whispered Arthur. 'It's you.'

Suddenly, Dragor appeared from the mouth of one of the other tunnels. Blood was still seeping from the wounds that Gwinnie had inflicted on him earlier. 'Those children are inside here somewhere,' he bellowed angrily to Morgana.

'Then there's no time to lose!' she replied, taking something out from beneath her cloak.

Instantly, Gwinnie recognized what it was. 'Pendragon's Belt!' she gasped.

With heavy steps, Dragor began to make his way over the planks of the rope bridge towards the island. In his hand swung the huge, spiked, metal mace. The bridge creaked and swayed as he walked.

'Dragor!' shouted Luke, leaping to his feet.

Dragor stopped. Morgana looked round to see where the voice had come from.

'What are you going to do, Luke?' whispered Gwinnie.

'I don't know,' replied Luke. 'But I'll think of something.'

17. DUEL ON THE BRIDGE

Luke stepped out of the tunnel and on to the stone bank.

'Luke Lancelot,' spat Morgana. 'We meet again!'

'What happened to you?' shouted Luke over the lava. 'I thought Mandrake killed you.'

'He very nearly did,' replied Morgana. 'Look!'

As she raised her hands, Luke could see that they were scarred with terrible burns. But when she pulled back the hood of her cloak,

Luke gasped in horror. The skin on her face
looked almost as though it had melted and
half-slid off her bony skull. Her hair was
matted into a coarse mess at the back of her
head and, where one of her eyes had once
been, there was simply a dark, empty socket.

'Remember, Luke, what I was holding in my
hand when Mandrake tried to kill me? That
bottle? The antidote to the poison I had used
on Arthur? When Mandrake blasted his fiery
breath at me, the bottle shattered, releasing

the magic inside it. Fortunately for me it was powerful magic. Just powerful enough to keep me alive. Just powerful enough to let me disappear into the smoke and be gone. Gone – but not dead. Unlike Mandrake. What a brother he turned out to be! Ah . . . I see you have met my other brother, Dragor.'

Luke glanced at Dragor, whose mace was swaying menacingly by his side.

'Yes,' said Luke. 'You have quite a family, Morgana. How did you get the belt?'

Morgana smiled. 'Oh, your little friend Percival was stupid enough to believe that if he brought me the belt then I wouldn't force him to take part in my little experiment.'

'Little experiment?' Luke asked.

'You see this tablet?' said Morgana, pointing towards a slab of stone beside the treasure. 'Let me read it to you . . .

'"If to stone you won't be turned
Heed well what I have taught:
He who takes the treasure
Must be pure in deed and thought.
But he who takes the belt complete
Will risk the mountain's ire,
For never shall it leave this place
Without a sea of fire."

'I'm trying to find a way to overcome the spell,' continued Morgana. 'Your little friends are helping me, but not one of them has yet survived. Some of them have got further than others, so there must be a way. And this belt, Luke —' she held the belt out in front of her — 'this belt brings its wearer everlasting life! I could live for ever, Luke!' she cackled. 'Think of that!'

Then she shook her head. 'But sadly we are running out of time,' she said. 'And I am running out of patience. I need that jewel in your father's hand, Luke . . . and you have arrived just in time to watch me get it!'

Morgana turned to Dragor who had now made his way over the bridge and on to the island.

'Smash him, Dragor!' commanded Morgana, pointing at the stone figure of Luke's father. 'Smash that stupid piece of stone!'

'No!' yelled Luke, drawing his sword and charging on to the rope bridge.

'Why try to save him, Luke?' sneered Morgana. 'Your father was a thief. A common, greedy, selfish thief! Look at him. He risked his family for a brooch. He can't have loved you very much, can he, Luke? A brooch! Oh no, he can't have loved you very much at all.'

'THAT'S NOT TRUE!' Luke shouted.

'Dragor,' commanded Morgana. 'Kill the boy!'

Dragor put down his mace and marched towards the bridge, drawing his sword. Luke grabbed on to the rope of the bridge and waited for Dragor to come at him.

Crash! Sparks flew into the air as their swords met. *Swoosh!* Dragor's sword sliced

through the air just in front of Luke's neck.

Luke summoned up all his courage and stepped forward, lunging at Dragor with his jewelled sword.

'Roooaaar!' Dragor blasted scorching flames towards Luke's face. Luke stepped back and – *crack!* – the wooden plank under his foot split and gave way beneath him.

'Aaagh!' yelled Luke as he fell through the bridge towards the boiling lava. Desperately trying to grab on to something, Luke felt his fingers close round a strand of rope. It stopped his fall just in time. Luke hauled himself back up on to the bridge, but Dragor was standing above him, sword in hand. He knocked Luke down again and grabbed his face with his craggy claws.

Slowly, Dragor began to push Luke's face over the edge of the bridge towards the boiling lava. 'You're going to die,' he said, smoke curling from his mouth. 'Just like your father. You're a coward, Luke, and your father was a coward too.'

Luke was trying frantically to cling on to the planks of the bridge, but Dragor was just too strong.

'Can you feel it, Luke?' said Dragor. 'Can you feel the heat?'

Luke's face was dripping with sweat as Dragor pushed it further towards the bubbling lava.

'Wait!' shouted a voice. It was Arthur.

'Arthur! No! What are you doing?' shouted Luke.

'You saved my life once,' said Arthur. 'Now it is my turn to save yours!'

Dragor looked up as Arthur leapt out of the tunnel and on to the stone bank. Quickly, Luke rolled away from Dragor's grip and jumped to his feet.

'Get off the bridge!' yelled Arthur.

'But you've only got a dagger!' Luke shouted back to him.

'It's all I need,' said Arthur. 'Get off the bridge now!'

Something in the tone of Arthur's voice made Luke do what he asked. 'Take my sword,' Luke said, stepping back on to the bank.

'Keep it,' Arthur replied. 'You may need it later. Trust me, Luke, I know what I'm doing.'

Slowly, Arthur stepped on to the bridge.

18. THE MAGIC
OF THE BELT

'I know how to do this, Morgana,' said Arthur,
walking carefully along the creaking bridge
towards the dragonman. 'Call off your
henchman, Dragor. I can release my father and
reverse the spell. The belt will be complete
and the spell will be broken. Everlasting life
will be yours, Morgana. Think of that!'

Morgana looked at Arthur suspiciously, but
Arthur could see the greed and the excitement
in her eyes. 'You tell me how first,' she said.

'Call him off, Morgana, or I'll cut the rope.'

Arthur held the blade of his knife against a thin strand of rope at the side of the bridge.

'You'll die if you cut the bridge,' said Morgana. 'You'll fall into the lava.'

'I am prepared for that,' Arthur replied. 'But if I cut this rope, Dragor dies as well. And you haven't got the strength to swing that mace, Morgana. You can't release the jewel on your own.'

Morgana looked at the heavy mace on the ground. 'All right,' she said. 'Get off the bridge, Dragor.'

Dragor stepped back on to the island where Morgana stood beside the treasure, his vicious eyes fixed on Arthur and his sword ready in his hand. Arthur followed.

'This had better be good,' said Morgana.

Arthur held out his hands. 'Give me the belt,' he said.

'Drop your weapon first,' barked Morgana.

'Throw it into the lava.'

Arthur tossed his dagger into the moat.
Morgana handed him the belt.

Slowly, Arthur approached the stone figure
of his father. He could make out every detail of
his face and he felt a longing to touch him, to
be held by his strong arms like he was all those
years ago when he was just a small child. How
he had missed him!

Tenderly, he took the belt and wrapped it
around the jewel in his father's hand, making

sure that the jewel sat right inside the hole in the buckle, from where it had come. He closed his eyes and furrowed his brow. He began to think hard – very hard.

At first, nothing happened. Then the treasure began to sparkle even more brightly than it had before – almost as if it were alive. There was a gentle, whistling sound as a warm, golden wind rose up from the middle of the treasure.

The wind circled around the stone walls of the chamber like a gleaming mist, lighting up the awestruck faces of Arthur, Luke and their enemies. Then it gathered and narrowed into a brilliant shaft of light before disappearing completely into the buckle of the belt in the stone knight's hand.

Everyone watched in silence to see what would happen next. Slowly, the stone began to change colour. It lost its hardness and all

Arthur could do was to stare wide-eyed and
open-mouthed in wonder as his own father
turned from solid grey stone back to living
flesh once more.

'Father,' he gasped. 'Father, you're alive!'

The knight moved his head, blinked and
stretched out his fingers. 'Father . . .' he
stammered. 'You called me father. Are you . . .
could you possibly be . . . my son . . . my . . .
Arthur?'

'I am,' replied Arthur.

'He's alive!' Morgana shrieked in delight. 'You've done it. You've broken the spell! You've reversed it! Now give me the belt.'

'Morgana, the belt belongs here,' said Arthur, 'with the treasure.'

'It belongs with me!' snapped Morgana. 'Dragor – the father!'

Dragor raised his sword and marched towards the knight.

'No,' said Arthur. 'Stop. Don't harm him. Morgana, if I give you the belt, will you let us all go free?'

'Once I'm safely across the bridge, I will let you go,' said Morgana. 'One false move from any of them, Dragor, and you kill them all!'

19. A White Wind

Arthur took the belt and the jewel from his father's hands and held them out to Morgana. Her eyes shining with greed, Morgana snatched them.

Morgana made her way off the island and over the fragile bridge as quickly as she could. Back on the island Dragor stood over Arthur and his father, brandishing his sword.

Morgana was soon over the bridge and on to the bank, where Luke waited helplessly. She turned to Luke. 'I'm going to have them killed anyway,' she whispered.

'You traitor!' yelled Luke. He ran straight on to the bridge and towards the island, towards his brother and father. His only thought was to save them – but he had played right into Morgana's hands.

'*Just* what I hoped you'd do!' she cackled. She was already sawing through one of the ropes that anchored the bridge to the stone bank with her dagger.

From the middle of the bridge, Luke looked back in horror. He wouldn't make it to the island *or* back to the bank before Morgana cut the rope.

'No!' shouted Arthur. 'Morgana, I beg you! NO!' With the bridge gone there would be no way out for any of them. Not Luke, not Arthur, nor their father.

Morgana looked across at Luke with an evil grin. 'Goodbye . . . Luke Lancelot!' she said.

'Goodbye . . . everyone!' And, with a final
twitch of her blade, the rope snapped and the
bridge went crashing down towards the lava
below.

'No!' cried Arthur, running towards the
moat. 'Luke! LUKE!'

Morgana fitted the jewel into the hole in the
buckle. 'Eternal life is mine!' she cackled. She

ran with the belt towards the entrance to one of the tunnels, turning only to shout over her shoulder to Dragor, 'Kill them all!'

Suddenly, a strange, whistling roar filled the chamber. It grew louder and louder. Soon it was a piercing howl. A swirling, blue-white wind rose up from the treasure. Arthur threw himself to the ground, covering his ears and his eyes. 'Turn away, Father!' he shouted. 'Close your eyes! Whatever you do, don't look at it!'

His father lay on the ground and covered his head with his hands.

The wind tore round the stone walls like a hurricane. Then it became a searing beam of light, whiter and brighter even than the sun – and it directed itself straight towards Morgana as she was escaping.

'No!' shrieked Morgana in terror. 'NO!' She tried to shield herself with her hand, but the light was too strong. As the beam entered her body, her movements became slow and heavy, as if she was wading through molten rock. And as the light disappeared into her she froze, with the belt in her hand, still and silent, into solid stone, her face set in an open-mouthed, terrified scream.

20. THE FINAL BATTLE

As quickly as the wind had risen, it died down again and disappeared back into the treasure.

Arthur leapt to his feet as Dragor came at him, sword in hand, raging with anger. 'What have you done to her?' he roared. 'What have you done to my sister? You'll pay for this!'

Arthur rushed to his father's side and drew the sword from his scabbard. He ran at Dragor, swinging his father's sword wildly, fearless with rage. Dragor fought back. Soon they were locked in a vicious duel, metal crashing against metal, knowing that, this time, only one of them would survive.

Flames spewed from Dragor's mouth as he slashed wildly at Arthur, beating him back with vicious blows right to the edge of the moat. Then, with a fearsome slash, he knocked Arthur's sword clean out of his hand. It spun through the air over the moat, before disappearing beneath the surface of the boiling lava. Arthur had nothing left to defend himself with.

'Gwinnie!' Arthur shouted. 'Gwinnie, where are you?' But there was no reply.

Arthur was cornered against the very edge of the moat. Desperately, he tried to run past Dragor, but Dragor caught him with a blow of his shield and Arthur was knocked to the ground behind him. Dragor turned to face him from the edge of the moat. 'Goodbye, Sir Arthur!' he bellowed, raising his sword high above his head.

Just as Dragor was about to swing his sword down and end Arthur's life, a hand appeared over the side of the moat. It was Luke's! He had managed to cling on to the remnants of the bridge as it crashed towards the lava. He had hauled himself up the ropes, and now he grabbed Dragor's ankle and pulled hard. Dragor stumbled, lost his balance and fell, with a roar, towards the lava.

Dragor flailed wildly. He grabbed a rope in his sharp claws and stopped his fall just before he hit the boiling lava.

Looking up he saw Luke, still hanging from the fallen bridge. Dragor began to climb up the rope. He was strong and soon he was right below Luke. He stretched up and grabbed Luke's foot with a scaly hand.

Frantically, Luke tried to kick him away, but the splintered plank that he was now holding on to gave way and Luke slipped further down the broken bridge.

The lava bubbled beneath them like a sea of fire.

Dragor blasted flames at Luke and pulled at his leg once more. This time, Luke twisted his foot from Dragor's grip and kicked with all the strength he had left. Dragor lost his hold and slipped. He grasped a thin strand of rope right at the bottom of the bridge. But the rope was weak and, with Dragor's weight, it began to twist and fray.

'No!' yelled Dragor as he watched the rope get thinner before his eyes. 'Help me!'

Luke looked at Dragor with narrowed eyes. This dragonman hanging on to the rope . . . *This* was the beast that was going to kill his father. Luke drew his sword and, with one swift blow, he chopped the rope.

With a piercing roar, Dragor plunged into the red-hot lava. Luke watched until he had

completely disappeared then, slowly, he began to climb up what was left of the bridge.

'Rooooaaaar!' There was another terrifying howl. Dragor's head, hideously burnt and melting, burst from the surface of the lava. Flames billowed from his mouth as, with one final desperate lunge, he tried to grab Luke's ankle.

Luke kicked his hand away but, as he did so, he lost his grip on the bridge. It was all he could do to grab the very last strand of rope.

Dragor slipped back beneath the surface of the lava, but Luke was dangling just inches above it. Sweat was pouring from his face. He was exhausted.

Arthur was at the edge of the moat. 'Come on, Luke,' he urged. 'Climb up! You can do it!'

With weary, shaking limbs, Luke began to climb up the bridge. But the bridge was getting weaker and weaker. Suddenly, a whole side of it gave way and crashed into the moat below. There was only one rope left, which Luke was hanging on to as tightly as he could. But it was fraying and splitting. Luke didn't know if he could make it to the top before it broke.

'Come on, Luke!' shouted Arthur. 'Take my hand!'

Luke reached up towards Arthur. He stretched out his fingers, but Arthur's hand was just too far away. 'I can't make it!' he shouted in despair as the rope frayed and slipped again.

'You can, Luke! You *can*! Just one more time! Reach up! You can do it!' Arthur was leaning over the edge of the moat as far as he could. His face was scorching with the heat and his hands and fingers were slippery and dripping with sweat.

Luke summoned all his strength and lunged

towards Arthur. Just as the rope snapped in his hand, Luke felt Arthur's fingers tighten round his own. He was safe.

21. THE SEA OF FIRE

With Arthur's help, Luke scrambled back over the edge of the moat and on to the island. But the bridge was gone. They were stranded.

'What's happened to Gwinnie?' asked Luke.

'I don't know,' Arthur replied. 'I left her at the mouth of the tunnel.'

The boys strained their eyes towards the many tunnel entrances on the other side of the moat, but there was no sign of her anywhere.

'Look!' said Arthur. 'The lava . . . I think it's getting angry!'

The rumbling inside the chamber was very loud now. The lava was bubbling more ferociously than before.

'It's going to erupt,' shouted Arthur over the noise. 'The volcano's going to erupt!'

Then he turned to his father. 'Quick! Put the brooch back with the treasure,' he said. 'It's our only hope of releasing the knights!'

The knight did as his son asked. Almost immediately, another sound filled the mountain: a strange, haunting sigh. The room filled with ghostly figures: spirits drifting and circling like vapour. As Luke watched them, he recognized faces. Faces of the spirits they had seen drifting on the Lake of Souls. They had come to return to the bodies of the stone knights that they had left as they froze, lifeless, inside the mountain.

'Drop the treasure!' Arthur shouted as the knights began to appear, flesh and bone again, at the entrances to the tunnels. 'Drop the treasure and run! Don't take it with you or you'll turn to stone again! Run! The volcano's going to erupt!'

The knights dropped the treasure and began to run down the tunnels, away from the Room of Fire.

The lava was bubbling and boiling so wildly now that the sound was almost deafening. A glob of red-hot rock spewed from the moat and landed smoking and fizzing beside Luke's feet.

'What shall we do?' yelled Luke to his brother. 'There's no way over the moat. We're trapped!'

Suddenly, Luke heard the galloping of hooves on stone – and Gwinnie, mounted on Avalon's back, burst through the entrance of one of the tunnels. Avalon spread his wings and flew over the lava on to the island in the middle.

'You did it, boy!' shouted Gwinnie into his ear, hugging him with pride and delight. 'You made it all the way!'

Then she turned to her brothers and her father. 'Quick! Get on! There's no time to lose!'

They all climbed on to Avalon's strong back. Luke took the reins and Avalon flew over the moat and back towards the tunnel.

'Which way?' shouted Luke. 'How do we find our way out of here?'

'Follow the sand!' yelled Gwinnie. 'I laid a trail of sand from the entrance into the mountain to here!'

'You're brilliant, Gwinnie!' Luke shouted back with a smile.

'No, Avalon's brilliant,' she replied. 'He found the courage to fly over the Lake of Souls to rescue us and now there's no stopping him!'

Avalon whinnied with pride and galloped into the tunnel, following the trail of sand.

Just then, the rumbling turned to a deafening roar and a huge explosion rang through the mountain. There was a burst of bright orange light, and Luke looked back to see a sea of boiling lava cascading towards them.

'Come on, boy!' Luke urged. 'Come on, Avalon. You can do it!'

Avalon was charging down the tunnel as fast as he could. But as fast as Avalon could gallop, the lava was moving faster, tumbling and pouring down the tunnel, towards them.

Luke looked over his shoulder again. The lava was closer now. Then closer still . . . It was about to catch them.

Just in time, Avalon burst out of the tunnel into the open air. He spread his mighty wings and soared up into the sky.

Luke looked below him at the rivers of red-hot rock surging out of the mountain and sliding like giant orange snakes into the lake around it. Then a great sea of molten lava spurted through the top of the volcano and poured in flaming torrents down the sides.

As they flew over the lake, Luke could see all the other knights they had rescued. Some were rowing in the long, narrow boats that had been hidden in the reeds on the island; others were swimming. All of them were making their way safely to the shore on the other side.

'We've done it!' shouted Luke.

'Hooray!' shouted Arthur to his father. 'We rescued you! We got you out alive! You're coming home!'

'I can't believe it's you!' their father shouted back. 'I never thought I would see any of you again. Never!'

Gwinnie just held her father tightly round the waist and closed her eyes. It was enough for her to know that they were together at last.

As they flew over the forest, Luke turned to Arthur. 'How did you do that thing with the belt?' he asked. 'How did you know it was going to work?'

'I didn't,' said Arthur with a smile, 'but it was worth a try. The spell said "he who *takes* the treasure . . ." would be turned to stone, so I closed my eyes and just kept repeating in my head that I wasn't going to *take* the treasure. I was doing the opposite. I was going to *return* it. So I thought the spell might do the opposite too – turn stone back to living flesh. When it worked, Morgana thought I had broken the spell, but I hadn't. I was just working *with* it. She wanted so much to believe that she could have that belt and get out alive, so I just helped her to believe it!'

'Genius!' said Luke, laughing at the cleverness of his brother. 'Come on, Avalon, I can see the towers of Camelot in the distance!'

22. THE RETURN

Avalon landed at the gates of Camelot and Luke, Arthur, Gwinnie and their father all dismounted.

Merlin was there to greet them. 'My brave knights,' he said with arms outstretched. 'Welcome! I knew you could do it. Strong and true. All of you – strong and true!'

He turned to the children's father. 'And you, my friend, it's good to have you back.' He put his arms round the knight and embraced him. 'My dear friend, Lancelot!'

Luke looked at his brother and sister,

wide-eyed with surprise. Lancelot! Their father
was Sir Lancelot! Of course. Now it all made
sense. That's why Merlin had given him the
knight's name Luke Lancelot on their last
adventure. Merlin had told him that it was the
name of a very brave knight he knew long ago
– but little did Luke know, until now, that this
knight was his father!

'Come,' said Merlin. 'A feast awaits you!'

Luke, Arthur, Gwinnie and their father all
followed Merlin into the Great Hall and up to
the Round Table.

As they took their places among old friends
– knights, ladies, squires and damsels – the
other knights they had rescued from the
mountain began to appear in the hall. There
was Gawain and Rufus and, behind them, their
old friend Percival.

Percival saw Luke and ran to his side. 'Oh,
Luke,' he said, 'I'm sorry. The belt . . . I was so

frightened . . . I thought . . .'

Luke raised his hand and put his arm round Percival's shoulder. 'I know,' he said gently. 'I know.'

Merlin stood beside the Round Table and banged his staff on the floor. A hush filled the room.

'Knights, ladies,' began Merlin, 'it is hard to know what to say. We have three heroes in our

midst. The three bravest members of the
Round Table I have ever known.'

Everyone in the hall began to cheer.

'They have rescued some of our best
knights. They have saved many lives and, for
that, no words that I can think of are good
enough to thank them.'

Everyone was now on their feet, clapping
and cheering and smiling at Luke, Arthur and
Gwinnie.

'But I am sure,' began Merlin again, 'that
you will all find your own ways of showing
your gratitude. In the meantime, Luke, Arthur,
Gwinnie, we have a feast to enjoy. The greatest
feast that Camelot has ever seen!'

Merlin banged his staff again and servants
scurried into the hall, their arms laden with
dishes of the most delicious-looking food that
the knights had ever set eyes on.

As the feast began, Luke turned to Merlin.

'There's one thing I don't understand,' he said.

'Go on,' said Merlin.

'If my father was so strong and true,' said Luke, 'why did he try to take the brooch?'

'It was for your mother,' said Merlin. 'He wanted to give it to her as a present; as a token of his love. But it was a bad choice, Luke. It shows you one thing, though . . .'

'What's that?' asked Luke.

'Not one of us is perfect,' replied Merlin. 'We all have our weaknesses. That is what makes us human. It is learning to overcome them that is the true test of our strength.'

Merlin looked at Luke with his bright, twinkling eyes. 'Come on,' he said. 'Eat up! This feast is for you. You have found your treasure!'

'Found my treasure?' said Luke, suddenly alarmed. 'What do you mean? We had to leave the treasure in the volcano, Merlin. I thought

you knew that.'

'Oh, I knew that all right,' said Merlin with a smile. 'And that's exactly where it should have been left. But you've got your father, Luke. Your family is going to be together again. Isn't that the greatest treasure you can have?'

'You're right,' said Luke, suddenly understanding Merlin's words. He thought of the smile there would be on his mother's face as he, Arthur and Gwinnie returned home with Lancelot, their father; her long-lost, beloved husband. 'The greatest treasure of all!'